Warrior Kids:

Pull No Punches

by
Mark Robson

First published in Great Britain in 2015
By Caboodle Books Ltd
Copyright © Mark Robson

A Catalogue record for this book is available from the British Library.

ISBN 978-0-9929389-7-0

Cover and Illustrations by Chie Kutsuwada

Printed by CPI Group (UK) Ltd, Croydon, CR0 4YY

The paper and board used in this book are natural recyclable products made from wood grown in sustainable forests. The manufacturing processes conform to the environmental regulations of the country of origin.

Caboodle Books Ltd.
Riversdale, 8 Rivock Avenue, Steeton BD20 6SA
www.authorsabroad.com

For all those who have helped at Daventry Tigers – especially Bethanie Tucker, without whom we would never have got started, and my first three brave young assistants: Abigail Faulkner, Megan Free and Ava Kempson, who have become indispensable! You all have my heartfelt thanks.

Acknowledgements

Many thanks again to my super editor, Jo Moult, and my number one proof-reader, Patrick Mahon. Your efforts make all the difference. Also, these books would not be the same without the wonderful illustrations by Chie Kutsuwada – thank you, Chie.

Contents

Chapter 1 – Nervous

Gurveer waited at his front gate, drumming his fingers against his leg and shivering. It was the big test this week – his first tae kwon-do grading. He had been practising like crazy over the weekend, but despite having gone over and over the exercises he was beginning to freak out. He tried to think of something funny to tell Donovan on the way to school. Normally corny jokes flowed in a constant stream from his mouth, but today it was as if someone had slammed the cover shut on the joke book inside his mind.

What's keeping him? he wondered, stamping his feet in an effort to warm them.

No matter how hard he tried, his mind just wouldn't focus. It was as if the bitter breeze had frozen his brain as well as his hands and feet. Maybe he should go back inside. Donovan would know to knock at the door, particularly in this weather. Gurveer's muscles felt tight, but his tension was as much from nervousness as from the temperature.

To his annoyance, his sister, Abhaya, and her friend, Gabriella, seemed to be looking forward to the exam. This didn't surprise Gurveer, but it was irritating. Abi liked challenges and she always did well in tests. As for Gabriella, she appeared to be permanently cheerful. Donovan was so good at tae kwon-do that he had nothing to worry about, which left Gurveer feeling nervous and unready. He shivered again and clapped his hands together several times.

'Come on, Donovan!' he muttered through chattering teeth. 'Hurry up! If you don't get here soon, I'm going to freeze to death!'

*   *   *   *   *

'Hey, posh boy! Got me a Christmas present yet?'

'The name is Donovan, Zach. And you lot might want to check behind you before you try anything stupid.'

Zach and his small group of friends turned to see what Donovan was talking about, and in that split-second Donovan darted away. He was far fitter now than he had been three months ago when Zach and his mates had first started bullying him. There were few in the school who could match Donovan at running now.

Ever since Donovan had hit Zach with a well-aimed punch, the bully had been wary. Now he didn't

8

approach Donovan unless he had his gang around him. Donovan had no intention of hitting him again, but Zach didn't know this. That one punch had got him into trouble with his teacher, his head teacher, his parents, and worst of all, Kai Green, his tae kwon-do instructor. That one uncontrolled moment of anger had nearly cost him his martial arts lessons. The last thing he wanted was to be excluded from his tae kwon-do club because of Zach.

Donovan sprinted away, using the element of surprise to get a head start. The cold air burned his face numb as he raced along the pavement, eyes scanning for any warning glint of ice.

'After him!' he heard Zach yell. Donovan heard the patter of the boys' footsteps as they began to follow. They were unlikely to catch him now. He didn't need to see the square, thuggish face of Zach to know that it would be burning a fierce shade of furious at having being fooled by such an old trick. There was no way that stocky Zach could outrun Donovan. Three months of training at tae kwon-do together with daily exercise had made him faster and stronger. Any danger would come from the other gang members.

Running the half mile along Church Street at speed, he turned down a side alley to cut through to West Street. His footsteps sounded strangely loud as he dodged between the bins. A cat gave a startled yowl before streaking ahead of him like a furry bullet.

The clattering echo of chasing feet was suddenly all round him, but it was hard to tell if they were gaining. As he reached the far end, Donovan turned left and saw Gurveer waiting for him as usual outside his front gate.

The sudden movement caught Gurveer's attention and he smiled as he saw Donovan run out from the alley.

'Morning, Donovan,' he called. 'Did you forget your homework and have to double back for it, or something?'

'Company,' his friend gasped, glancing over his shoulder as he approached. 'I was a bit late leaving today. Unfortunately that put me in the wrong place, at the wrong time.'

'Zach?'

'Who else?' Donovan grinned, momentarily putting his hands on his knees and bending over to catch his breath. Puffy clouds of white billowed from his mouth, rising up round his face as he panted. 'Not that he could catch me himself, but some of his friends are a bit quicker. Look. Here they come now. Let's go.'

The pursuing boys slowed to a walk when they saw that Donovan was no longer alone. Zach's gang of friends knew that he and Gurveer were studying martial arts and appeared wary of approaching them without their leader.

'I thought Zach had stopped bothering you,' Gurveer said, frowning as they strode away from the other boys at a fast pace. 'You should tell the teachers if he's up to his old tricks again.'

'This is the first time in a while that he's tried anything,' Donovan replied, giving a shrug as he calmed his breathing. 'Not sure what's brought it on today. Maybe he thinks he's kept his head down long enough. I think we'll avoid the alleys today. Let's take the main roads, shall we?'

'Lead on, dark warrior,' Gurveer said, giving him a mock salute.

Donovan's lips tightened into a thin line. 'I don't feel much like a dark warrior having just run away from Zach's mob,' he admitted, glancing over his shoulder at the gang of boys behind them. They were holding their distance and muttering to one another, unsure of what to do without Zach to goad them into action.

Gurveer shrugged. It seemed like only yesterday that their tae kwon-do instructor, Kai Green, had first told them the meanings of their names. He felt sure it was one of those life-changing moments that would live with him forever.

Kai had told them that Donovan was an Irish name meaning 'dark warrior', while his own name meant 'warrior of the guru'. His sister, Abhaya, and her friend, Gabriella, had also been named for warriors.

Kai seemed to think this was more than a simple coincidence. Some years ago he had travelled to the Far East to study martial arts. One of the masters who taught him there had predicted that one day four young warriors would come to Kai. This master had made him promise to teach them well, as they were destined to: '. . . *face dangers that would affect the fates of many*.' Gurveer still had no idea what this meant. He felt sure Kai knew more than he was telling, and the man seemed convinced that Gurveer and his friends were the four his master had talked about.

'You might not feel like a dark warrior now, but you will tonight,' Gurveer assured him.

'Tae kwon-do classes are fun,' Donovan replied. 'But I'm no more a dark warrior than you're a warrior of the guru! And it's the mock grading tonight, remember?'

'Tell me something I don't know!' Gurveer moaned. 'Worse – the real thing is only two days away.'

'Nervous?'

'Aren't you?' Gurveer asked.

'Not really,' Donovan answered, giving a shrug. 'I'll do my best. I can't do any more than that.'

'Yeah, well you make it look easy. Not all of us have your skill. I did have a great dream last night though.'

'Really? About tae kwon-do?'

'No. I dreamed I was the author of *The Hobbit* and everyone was treating me like royalty.'

'Cool . . . I think,' Donovan replied slowly, wondering what the punch line would be.

'Yeah. I was gutted when I woke up and realised I was just Tolkien in my sleep . . . talkin' in my sleep – get it?'

'That's awful!' Donovan groaned, slapping his forehead. 'And I really should have seen it coming.'

The whole prophecy thing that Kai had talked about sounded a bit far-fetched to Gurveer. When they'd started martial arts lessons, Donovan had been the only one facing obvious danger. Zach and his gang had picked him out to be a victim for their bullying. But dealing with Zach didn't seem to qualify as '*affecting the lives of many*'. It was true that about a month ago, the four of them had chased and caught one of three thieves who had just stolen goods from Mr Patchesa's corner shop, but even that hadn't felt heroic or life-changing.

'You're doing better than you think at tae kwon-do, you know,' Donovan said suddenly. 'You've improved a huge amount in the last few weeks. You'll get through the grading easily. Do you practise with Abi?'

'Sometimes,' Gurveer admitted. 'But more often on my own.'

'If you come round to mine tonight before class we can practise together if you like.'

'That would be great! Thanks. I'll be there.'

Donovan glanced over his shoulder. Zach had caught up with his gang and the boys were gaining on them without running. 'I think it's time we stepped on it. They're getting a bit too close for comfort.'

'Agreed. We don't want to be like clown fish.'

Donovan looked at him confused. 'I probably shouldn't ask,' he said. 'But you've got me again. Clown fish?'

'It's a clown fish saying . . .' Gurveer replied, grinning. 'Keep your friends close, but your anemones closer!'

Donovan gave another exaggerated groan.

'You're right, he said. 'We don't want to do that!'

The two boys broke into a jog. The group behind them started jeering and Zach gave a strange, wheezing laugh. Gurveer glanced back again. Zach looked red in the face from running and, although his friends were laughing and jeering with him, Gurveer could see some of them glancing at Zach as they jeered. He got the impression that they were secretly laughing as much at Zach as they were at him and Donovan. His lips curled upwards into a smile at that thought.

Despite attempting to keep up his usual stream of jokes, Gurveer felt sick with worry. Kai had told them the man coming to test them at the grading later in the week was the top man in the Tae Kwon-Do

Association of Great Britain. What if the others passed and he didn't? Donovan wasn't going to fail – he was brilliant. To his annoyance, his sister and her friend were both better than he was as well.

School wasn't far away now. He could just see the gates up ahead. Since making friends with Donovan, Zach and his gang no longer scared him, though he was still wary of them. Zach wouldn't dare try anything this close to school. There were too many parents and teachers about. They were safe, but his stomach was still churning at the thought of the test.

If I'm this nervous about the grading now, what am I going to be like on Thursday? Gurveer wondered.

Chapter 2 – Watched

'I hate being watched,' Gurveer muttered as they waited outside the door to the Leisure Centre's sports hall that evening.

He looked across at the clock behind the reception desk. It was nearly six; almost time for the lesson.

'Kai watches us every week,' Donovan whispered back. 'I don't know what you're so wound up about.

'That's different,' he insisted. 'This is a test and I've always been rubbish at tests.'

Gurveer felt more than sick. His stomach felt like it was full of snakes trying to squirm their way free. His entire body felt taut as a guitar string and the sour taste of vomit haunted the back of his mouth. He'd tried stretching, but it hadn't helped. He fiddled with the knot on his white belt as he waited for the class to begin.

'Tests in school are different,' Donovan insisted, catching his attention again. 'That's maths 'n' literacy and stuff. You're not the only one who doesn't like being tested at that. You're good at this. You'll be fine,

Gurveer. You'll see. Besides, this is just the practice.'

'So you keep saying, but for some reason it isn't helping.'

Abi and Gee had their heads close together and they were also whispering to one another. Gee gave one of her trademark giggles. *Did she never stop giggling?* Gurveer wondered. It would be easy to underestimate her given the way she acted, but he knew that there was much more to Gabriella than her annoying laugh. She'd been hanging round Abi long enough that he knew she did some really cool stuff in the holidays, like rock climbing and mountain biking in the Pennines with her dad, so why did she act like she only had half a brain? Girls were a mystery; and those two more than most. They always had something to talk and laugh about. To his annoyance, judging by the way the girls kept glancing his way, he was pretty sure that right now they were laughing at him.

'OK, everyone,' Kai announced in a loud voice. 'Go in and make up the rows.'

'Yes, sir!' everyone chorused.

Gurveer hooked his bag over his shoulder and took a sip from his sports bottle, waiting for the others to go in first. Donovan waited with him. There was a short delay as everyone took turns to pause and bow as they went through the doorway, but when all the others had gone in there was no excuse to stay outside any more. Gurveer went to the door. As Donovan went ahead of him, he glanced round just in time to see a man wearing a long coat, dark sunglasses, a black scarf and black leather gloves coming through the automatic front doors of the Leisure Centre.

It was the dark, wrap-around sunglasses that made Gurveer pause for just a fraction of a second before bowing and continuing into the hall. It was dark outside. Why would anyone wear sunglasses in the dark? *A strange man for sure*, he thought.

Like the others, he paused to bow as he entered. Donovan was right. Being nervous tonight was stupid! Why was he so scared? Kai had entered him for the test. Even if he messed up the pretend grading tonight it didn't matter. It was Thursday that counted. *Unless I'm so bad that Kai decides not to let me take the test after all*, Gurveer thought, his mind spiralling towards panic once more. *I couldn't bear it if the girls got promoted and I didn't. It would be soooooo embarrassing!*

The others were all making up the lines ready to start the class. He had to focus. Running to the far side of the hall, he put his bag and sports bottle down, took off his trainers, socks and wrist watch and ran back to take his place on the back row.

'Class cheryots! Kyung ye.'

Kai called the orders for the class to come to attention and bow. Gurveer could barely breathe as he waited for the class to begin. Something – a feeling – made him look up to the glass windows of the first floor café above the training area. To his surprise, he saw the man in the sunglasses was sitting at a table next to the windows gazing down at him. A chill ran down Gurveer's spine.

'Chunbi!'

Without thinking, Gurveer automatically moved his left foot out and placed his hands in front of his belt as Kai gave the 'ready' order. He had to pay attention, he realised. Listening to Kai was more important than jumping at shadows.

'Those of you who have done gradings before know what to expect,' Kai began. 'For the benefit of our beginners, the way a tae kwon-do grading runs is this: first I will bring the class to attention, introduce the examiner, and then dismiss you all to sit at the back of the hall and wait for your turn to be tested. Sit there quietly. I don't want to hear any talking. When I call out your name . . .'

The briefing went on for some time, but no matter how hard Gurveer tried to listen, his mind kept wandering. Abi would tease him if she passed and he didn't. Gurveer could see her out of the corner of his eye. She was soaking up Kai's instructions. He had to listen – *Concentrate!* he told himself.

'. . . and then you will be asked to move over to a table at the side of the gym where you will be asked a few basic questions. Is everyone clear about what they have to do?'

'Yes, sir!' the host of students replied.

Gurveer said the words with the others, but inside his panic was growing like the darkness before a storm. Did he really know what he was doing? Suddenly, he felt as if he knew nothing.

'And remember – there will be students from Mr Cotter's club here grading as well, so I expect you to look sharp – not just for the examiner, but to show those other guys that we're the best club in the area. Understood?'

'Yes, sir!'

'OK, everyone move to the back of the hall and sit down on the floor so we can begin.'

As he turned to do as he was told, Gurveer glanced up to the glass wall of the café again. The man in the dark glasses was still there . . . still watching, but even as Gurveer looked up at him, the man pushed his chair back, got to his feet and moved away out of sight towards the exit.

Strange! It's almost as if I scared him away by looking at him, Gurveer thought. *Oh for goodness' sake! Stop daydreaming and focus, Gurveer! He's gone. Now concentrate and listen.*

Chapter 3 – Orders

Kicking his heels as he ambled homeward, Gurveer gradually fell further behind the girls as he replayed the mock exam in his mind. Donovan had raced off on his bike, leaving him to chew over his performance alone. He was head down and lost in thought as he turned into the alley. There was no warning. No sound. No sense of movement. The first he knew was when the gloved hand clamped across his nose and mouth and he was pulled suddenly backward.

'Don't struggle,' a man's voice whispered close to his ear. 'I don't want to have to hurt you.'

The man hooked his other wrist under Gurveer's chin, forcing his head up and restricting his breathing even further. Gurveer's heart hammered in his chest and he felt a burning sensation in his stomach. The man felt strong – far too strong for him to break free. The smell of leather filled his nostrils as he struggled to breathe.

'I didn't want to have to do this,' the whispering voice continued. 'But I need you to understand that

you can say nothing of my presence to Kai. I will know if you talk to him, do you understand?'

Gurveer didn't have to see the man to know it was the person he had seen watching them at the Leisure Centre. He tried to nod. His head didn't move, but the man clearly felt the pressure of his effort.

'Good,' he said, adjusting his hand slightly to allow Gurveer to breathe through his nose. 'Very sensible. Keep quiet and there will be no trouble. Blab and you will disappear and never be seen again. Have I made myself clear?'

Again, Gurveer tried to nod.

'Good. Forget your promise and it will be the last thing you do.'

Before Gurveer could so much as flinch, the man's wrist was removed from across his throat and he was shoved forward. He fell, putting his hands out to break his fall. Pain exploded in his palms as he hit the ground hard and rolled over. Struggling to his feet, he looked for his attacker, heart still pounding and throat dry. Nothing. He listened hard, but all he could hear was the sound of the girls chatting towards the far end of the alleyway. A shiver ran up and down his back. Gurveer had never been particularly afraid of the dark before, but the man had been like a shadow: dark, silent and horribly scary.

Stumbling away at speed, he scrambled to catch up with Abi and Gee.

* * * * *

Driss rapped twice on the solid wooden door. There was a pause.

'Come in!'

The order was firm and commanding. Driss took a deep breath. Gripping the handle tightly to stop his fingers from shaking he opened the door and bowed before walking in.

'Master,' he began. 'The four you instructed me to watch will take their first martial arts exam tonight.'

Driss always felt nervous when meeting the leader of COBRA. This man was dangerous and difficult to please. Wise men did not upset him. It had been noted that people who made him angry sometimes had unfortunate 'accidents' afterwards.

'And how are the *children* doing?' the master replied, his voice sounding as poisonous as the snakes that lived in the tanks lining every wall of the huge third-floor office. 'Are there any signs?'

Hesitating a moment, Driss struggled to choose words that would not provoke anger.

'They are learning quickly, master,' he said. 'But not unusually so. Since the incident last month when they chased the shoplifter, I have not noticed them do anything special.'

'And all they did then was to chase another boy

down some streets and corner him. Hmm, it appears to be as I suspected . . .' the figure replied, '. . . a false alarm. However, Master Lin has a reputation for being strangely accurate with some of his predictions, so let's not be hasty in leaping to conclusions.'

He got to his feet and walked from behind his huge oak desk across the plush, blood-red carpet to one of the glass tanks. As he approached, the cobra coiled inside reared its head and flared its hood, hissing a warning not to come any closer.

'She's not settled yet,' he muttered. He glanced across at Driss. 'My new arrival,' he explained in a louder voice. 'She's still on edge in her new home.'

As I would be living near you, thought Driss, unnerved not so much by the presence of so many poisonous snakes as he was by the reputation of the man who owned the building. Deadly though they were, he would rather anger the snakes than he would their owner.

As the man touched the glass of the tank the cobra struck, recoiling as it impacted the glass wall. Not flinching in the slightest at the attack, he slowly removed his finger and a tiny dribble of venom trickled down the inside of the glass where the snake had attempted to bite him.

Driss shuddered and watched as his master bent over to better observe the snake's movements.

'Keep watching them for now,' the man ordered without looking round. 'Let me know if anything changes.'

'Yes, Master,' Driss replied.

'Is there anything else?'

Driss hesitated a moment. Should he say anything about having to scare the boy after class a couple of days ago? No, he decided. The Master would not be impressed that he had been seen. Better to keep quiet.

'No, Master,' he said.

'Good. Go! Don't let me down, Driss.'

'No, Master.'

*　*　*　*　*

'And what would sir like for his tea this special night?'

'Mum!' Gurveer drawled, rolling his eyes at her.

'Would sir like some of my nice homemade Rogan Josh? Or should I do a quick run to the fish and chip shop?'

'Sir would like his mother to stop being silly and talk properly,' Gurveer replied, dumping his school bag on a kitchen chair and giving her a quick hug.

His hands still stung from where he had grazed them on the ground in the alley on Tuesday, but they were healing fast. He felt guilty for not telling his mum and dad about the encounter, but just the thought of telling them made his heart start thumping. It was one thing to have parents and teachers tell him about 'stranger danger', but the reality was nothing like he had imagined. The man's threat to make him disappear was too immediate and real for him to ignore. It was as if the man's words had gagged him. Strangely, he felt even worse for not telling Kai and Donovan.

I'll tell her, he thought, opening his mouth ready to tell the story. *It's the right thing to do.*

Abi entered the room behind him. 'Did someone say fish and chips?' she asked.

Gurveer shut his mouth. The opportunity had gone. There was no way he was going to say anything in front of his sister. She would blab it to everyone.

'Better still would be pizza!' Abi continued enthusiastically.

'Eurghh! Just the thought of all the grease is turning my stomach,' Gurveer complained. 'Can I eat after the grading, Mum? I'm not sure I can manage anything just now. I've got pre-test nerves.'

'You ought to eat something to give you strength,' she insisted.

'Maybe a sandwich or something then,' he said. 'Just a snack. No more.'

'Very well, Gurveer,' she agreed. 'But don't complain to me afterwards that you had no energy during the test.'

'Actually, I fancy some of your Rogan, Mum,' Abi said, sniffing the air appreciatively. 'It smells great, as always. Are you coming to watch tonight?'

'Of course!' she replied. 'I wouldn't miss it. Dad's going straight to the Leisure Centre from work. He should also be there in time to see you.'

'Thanks, Mum!'

'Your uniforms are ironed and on your beds, but eat and freshen up before you change. You don't want food stains on those white suits tonight.'

Even a sandwich proved too much for Gurveer. He chewed the first mouthful round and round, but his mouth was so dry he couldn't swallow it. In the end he had to take a drink of water to wash the sticky bread paste down. It landed like a lead weight in his stomach, which instantly began tumbling it round and round like a washing machine.

To his annoyance, he had to sit and watch as his sister ate her curry, smiling and chatting about her day at school the whole time. Didn't she care about tonight, or was she really so confident that she felt no nerves? It wasn't fair, he decided. Abi seemed able to live up to her name, Abhaya, which meant 'fearless', yet he felt nothing like the warrior he'd been named after. Weren't warriors meant to be brave too?

Chapter 4 – The Grading

The first person Gurveer saw as he entered the training hall that evening was Donovan. His friend looked completely at ease. The atmosphere was charged with excitement and nervous energy. A buzz filled the air, but no one looked like he felt. He scanned the hall and the windows of the café that overlooked it for any sign of the mysterious stranger. If he was there, Gurveer could not see him. His focus switched back to the other students.

Is it only me who's feeling terrible, or is everyone else just better at hiding it? Gurveer wondered.

He tried jogging on the spot to loosen off the tightness in his body, but he didn't do it for long. The motion unsettled his stomach more than ever.

'Come on Gurveer!' he muttered to himself. 'You can do this. Calm down. How hard can it be? You know the exercises. You know the theory.'

Abi and Gee were stretching and Donovan was talking with one of the older children. He was laughing. How could Donovan laugh?

There were lots of unfamiliar faces, many busy practising patterns of moves, or doing warm-up exercises. Some looked serious and focused. Others were just going through the motions and chatting with their friends as they waited.

A double-length table had been set up at the front of the hall and draped over it was a large maroon coloured cloth with a gold fringe and the TAGB insignia emblazoned in bright gold stitching in the middle. Gurveer noted another single table had been placed at the front right side of the hall with two chairs behind it. The theory test table, he realised. Would it be Kai asking the questions? He hadn't thought to ask.

All the black belts were wearing black blazers with a golden badge sewn on to the left breast pocket, black trousers, white shirts and identical ties. They all looked very smart.

'Students, make the rows up!' ordered Kai in a loud voice. 'Parents and friends, please take your seats at the back of the hall.

'Good luck, Gurveer. Good luck, Abi,' their mother called in an embarrassingly loud voice.

Gurveer nodded to her and did his best to smile. He took his position with the other white belts at the very back of the rows. There was some shuffling as people found their places. Then suddenly everyone was still.

'Class, cheryots!' Kai ordered, his voice carrying loud and clear across the hall.

As one, the class stood to attention, straight and tall.

'Kyung ye! Ladies and gentlemen, I would like to welcome our grading examiner for tonight, 9th Degree black belt and Chairman of the . . .'

Gurveer eyed the examiner. He looked old and poker-faced, with a barrel chest and a little more weight around his middle than Gurveer expected of a Grand Master. Dressed as he was in a dark blazer and tie, it was hard to picture this man as an accomplished martial artist, yet he must have been doing tae kwon-do for a long time to have reached the very highest grade of black belt. And you didn't reach 9th Dan by being average.

'Class, cheryots! Dismiss! Go and sit at the back of the hall quietly and wait to be called forward.'

Gurveer, Donovan and the two girls sat together on the floor in silence. The sudden increase in tension in the hall bizarrely made Gurveer feel slightly better. The fact that others were finally beginning to look more nervous gave him a boost. He could feel himself stiffening again and he gripped the ends of his belt to stop his hands from shaking. The pain of the pressure against his grazed palms helped him to focus.

'Anthony Bridges, position one,' Kai called out, pointing to a marker on the floor.

'Yes, sir!' a boy sitting not far to Gurveer's right shouted back. He got to his feet and ran across to the spot, came to attention, bowed and adopted a ready position.

'Abhaya Chaudhry, position two.'

'Yes, sir!'

This is it, Gurveer thought. *My turn next.*

'Gurveer Chaudhry, position three.'

'Yes, sir!'

Gurveer was on his feet and running. He arrived at his spot so quickly, he struggled to stop. *Attention . . . bow . . . ready!* he thought, following the protocol they had learned.

'Gabriella Fletcher, position four.'

Donovan was called, and directed to begin a second line behind the first. Three further white belt students were called to complete the second row.

'Name and rank by position!' the examiner called.

Starting at position one and working up, each student raised their right hand, declared their name and added '. . . tenth kup, sir!' on the end. With the formalities out of the way, the grading began.

Press ups, sitting stance punches, leg raising exercises, stepping forward and backwards, punching and blocking. Before Gurveer realised what was happening they were performing Sajo Jirugi – the four-directional blocking and punching exercise they had been practising for weeks and weeks.

'Cheryots! Kyung ye! Move to the side for your theory questions.'

Was that it? Gurveer thought, astonished. *It was all over so quickly. Just the theory to go and I know that inside out. What was I so worried about?*

A few simple questions later and the theory test was over as well.

'That wasn't so bad, was it?' Donovan whispered to him as they returned to their places.

'No. I guess not,' Gurveer replied, feeling weak with relief that it was all over.

He watched as the higher belt students were put through their paces: patterns, set-sparring, complicated combinations of moves that made what he had been asked to do look like child's play. The seniors were asked to put on their padded sparring gear and the free-sparring began.

'That looks so cool!' Donovan muttered. 'I can't wait to start doing that.'

'Those guys are not in the same league as Kai and other black belts though, are they?' Gurveer whispered back.

'No, but it looks like fun.'

'All that gear looks expensive,' Gurveer said. 'I'm not sure my mum and dad are going to be happy when they realise they are going to have to find even more money.'

'I'm going to put it on my Christmas and birthday

lists,' Donovan said, his lips tightening into a determined line. 'I sort of feel the more I get into this, the less likely my mum and dad will make me stop when my scholarship runs out.'

'Surely when they see you doing well at your gradings and practising all the time, they'll support you, won't they?'

Donovan shrugged. 'If they haven't got enough money, it will be hard,' he replied, watching as the students swapped round and began another bout.

The final group were called to the examiner's table for their questions, rather than the side table. They stood sweating and panting from their efforts, while the examiner fired questions at them. They had looked impressive, but they looked uncomfortable now that they had finished the practical.

It suddenly dawned on Gurveer that he had no idea how the gradings were scored. How had he done? He didn't remember doing anything wrong, but he didn't know what the examiner had seen.

Surely I've done enough to pass, he thought. *So long as I pass, I'll be happy with that.*

A sudden chill swept through Gurveer's body and instinctively he looked up at the café windows. To his horror, the man in the dark glasses was back . . . and looking right at him. He had a sudden urge to tell someone: his parents, Kai, to just shout out to the adults in the room . . . but before he could so much as make a move the man slowly shook his head. Gurveer froze.

It's as if he can read my mind, Gurveer thought a hard lump forming in his throat and an icy knot pulling tight in his stomach. *What can I do?*

Chapter 5 – A New Friend?

'Hi, Donovan. Hello, Gurveer. Can I join you?'

'Why, Marcus?' Donovan answered. 'What does Zach want now?'

Gurveer looked round the school playground for the bully and the rest of his gang. He was nowhere in sight, but that didn't mean he wasn't hidden, watching them. His eyes came back to rest on Marcus, who was looking uncomfortable.

Marcus wasn't skinny like Donovan, but neither was he carrying as much weight as Gurveer. His short, straw blonde hair was parted on the left and swept across his head with military neatness, and his bright blue eyes had a look of innocence about them.

'This is nothing to do with Zach,' Marcus offered. 'I'm finished with following him round. He's twisted.'

'We've noticed,' Gurveer said. 'But that hasn't stopped you from hanging out with him before.'

'Yeah, but I've had my Mum and Dad on my back ever since the shoplifting thing last month. They've been telling me I should get better friends. I'm

beginning to think they're right, that's all. I just want you to know there are no hard feelings about that, by the way.'

'Really? OK. So you've come to us. . .' Donovan said thoughtfully, observing the boy's face carefully for any sign of deceit. 'Tell him a joke, Gurveer.'

Gurveer had no idea why Donovan wanted him to tell a joke, but he rarely turned down an opportunity.

'What did the mayo say when someone opened the fridge, Marcus?'

Marcus thought for a moment.

'Dunno,' he said with a shrug.

'Close the door, I'm dressing,' Gurveer said with a grin.

'Um . . . yeah, right,' Marcus said, trying to smile politely.

'And another . . .' Donovan insisted.

'OK, why do you never see hippopotamuses hiding in trees?'

'No idea,' Marcus replied, waiting for the punchline.

Gurveer paused a moment for effect. 'Because they're really, REALLY good at hiding,' he said, laughing.

Marcus again forced a smile and nodded. 'Good one,' he said, though his voice told a different story.

'I believe him,' Donovan said suddenly, turning to Gurveer. 'If Zach had sent him, I think he'd have made more of an effort to laugh. No offense, Gurveer, but not many of your jokes are really laugh-out-loud funny.'

Gurveer wasn't sure what to say to that. He liked corny jokes – the cornier the better. He shrugged and looked at Marcus. The boy appeared unsure of himself. Donovan was right to wonder why Marcus had come to them. He and Donovan were hardly the cool kids.

'So what are you into, Marcus?' he asked.

'I like football, but I'm not really much good at it,' he admitted, sticking his hands in his pockets and looking down at his feet. 'I thought I might try this karate thing you do. I've always thought martial arts were pretty neat.'

'It's not karate. We do tae kwon-do,' Donovan corrected. 'It's similar in some ways, but . . . well, you'd be better talking to Kai than to us.'

'Kai?'

'Our instructor,' Gurveer explained. 'And yeah, it's fun. We took our first exam this week. I'm hoping we'll both be promoted at tomorrow's lesson.'

'Promoted?'

'Get a new colour belt. It'll be great if we passed. We'll get to learn all sorts of new stuff as yellow tags.'

'So do you have to fight much?' he asked.

'We haven't done any contact sparring yet. Eventually we will,' Donovan replied enthusiastically.

'We're still learning the basics right now, and the sparring they do in class isn't like a street fight. It's sort of an elaborate game of tig really, except you can only tig your opponent on certain parts of their body and you get more points for doing it with your feet than your hands.'

'So you don't get hurt?'

'Nobody beats us up in class, if that's what you mean.'

Marcus nodded, looking embarrassed.

'You have to work hard, and I won't lie to you – I've hurt afterwards,' Gurveer added. 'Not from being hit, but there've been days when I've got home from class with muscles hurting that I didn't know I had! I never thought I'd like a sport, but tae kwon-do's interesting and the instructor makes it fun.'

'And you learn to fight . . .'

'Yes,' Donovan said. 'But we're not allowed to use what we learn outside class.'

'You hit Zach . . .'

'I made a mistake,' Donovan admitted. 'It was the wrong thing to do. I got into a whole heap of trouble with just about every adult I know!'

'Sounds like me after I stole those sweets,' Marcus said, looking down at his feet. 'I knew it was wrong, but I did it anyway. I thought it was cool at the time – sort of exciting. It wasn't cool. It was stupid.'

'I guess we all get things wrong sometimes,'

Gurveer said, his thoughts flitting back to the stranger. *I wish I had the courage to do something about dark glasses guy,* he added in his mind. *I should tell Donovan . . . or Kai, but I can't – I just can't. Not after what he said to me.*

'Can you show me some of your tae kwon-do moves?' Marcus asked.

'Not here,' Donovan replied quickly, looking round as if even the mention of it might get him into trouble. 'We can practise at home, but not in school. Why don't you come to the Leisure Centre tomorrow and have a free trial lesson? We can introduce you to Kai, can't we, Gurveer?'

'Sure,' he replied, not really listening any more.

'You'll need to get your mum or dad to come along and sign a form before you can join in, but it would be good to have someone else from the school there.'

'I don't know if they'll let me,' he said.

'Well you won't know unless you ask.'

Chapter 6 – What's Wrong With Me?

'Hey, Donovan – how do you catch a bra?'

Donovan drew his eyebrows together slightly as he thought for a moment. Then he sighed, wondering just how bad this one was.

'I don't know, Gurveer. How do you catch a bra?'

'With a booby trap, of course!'

Gurveer was pleased to see his friend actually laugh at one of his jokes, but his heart wasn't really in it tonight. He looked round, searching the reception area to see if there was any sign of the man in the dark glasses. He was nowhere to be seen.

'By your standard, that's actually approaching funny,' Donovan admitted, chuckling. 'And look – there's Marcus. He showed up!'

Donovan lifted a hand in greeting and went to meet him. Gurveer watched as his friend introduced Marcus and his mother to Kai. Donovan returned to Gurveer with a big smile on his face.

'You know what? I wasn't totally sure before, but I think Marcus really is trying to be friends with us. He was certainly serious about having a go at tae kwon-do.'

The girls appeared from their changing rooms. For once Gabriella was not giggling. Gurveer was surprised to see her looking serious. Was she nervous about getting the results as well?

'Do you think we'll find out how we did tonight, boys?' Gabriella asked, brushing down the sides of her training suit.

'According to the senior students, Kai always hands out the belts and certificates at the first lesson after the grading,' Donovan said, rubbing his hands together excitedly.

'Trust you to know!' Abi laughed. 'You seem to know everyone in the club these days, Donovan.'

'I like the people here,' Donovan replied. 'They're easy to talk to. I think I have more friends here than I've got in school.'

'Well, starting at Oxtree in Year Six probably didn't help,' Gurveer suggested. 'And if Zach hadn't started picking on you so early, I think you would've made friends a lot more quickly.'

'Probably, but it doesn't matter. I'm happy enough now. Look. Kai has a big plastic bag with him. I bet that's the new belts.'

Gurveer felt a thrill run through his body. Kai was smiling. Surely he wouldn't look so happy if his students had not all done well. *But what if he's happy* *because **most** of his students have done well?* he thought. *Just because he's smiling doesn't mean **I've** passed.*

Suddenly, the nervousness that Gurveer had felt before the grading returned in full force. It combined with the fear he'd been masking about the watcher in black, whom he half expected to see walk in through the door at any second. A wave of dizziness hit him and he felt the familiar sick feeling rise in his stomach. His knees felt as if they might give way at any second.

'I'm just going to nip to the boys' room before we start,' he mumbled and turned away from the entrance to the training hall.

'Are you OK, Gurveer?' Abi asked. 'You don't look too good.'

'I'm fine,' he called back. 'I'll be through in a minute.'

He walked quickly round the corner to the dry locker room and through it to the toilets. To his complete relief there was no one else in there and he dashed into a cubicle and shut the door behind him. Leaning back against the door, he took several deep breaths. The combination of smells inside made his stomach churn even harder. The foul after-smell of someone's visit to the toilet was combined with the odour of sweaty clothing and someone's overuse of a scented anti-perspirant.

The brew was too much. He tried to open the door again and get to somewhere with fresher air, but he wasn't quick enough. Before he knew it he was bent over the toilet and throwing up into the bowl. He retched twice . . . three times . . . four. Then the wave of sickness passed and his legs felt weaker than ever. Pulling some toilet tissue from the holder, he wiped his mouth clean, pulled the flush handle and staggered out of the cubicle and across the tiled floor towards the sinks.

Splashing cold water over his face made him feel much better. Cupping his hands under the tap, he sucked water into his mouth, swilled it round and spat it back out into the sink. After a moment's pause he rubbed his cheeks with the palms of his hands and looked up at his reflection in the mirror. Although he still felt awful, he didn't look too bad.

The others would all be starting the training session about now. Would Kai run the lesson first and then hand out the belts, or do the presentation at the beginning? He didn't know.

'Come on, Gurveer!' he urged softly. 'You did all right at the test. Forget about dark glasses guy. Maybe he won't show tonight.'

He pushed away from the sink and dried his hands and face with the air drier on the wall before heading back out along the corridor to the reception area. Everyone had gone into the hall. Gurveer crossed to the door and peered in through the window. Kai caught sight of him and waved him in.

'Take your place, Gurveer,' the instructor ordered. 'Quickly!'

Gurveer ran to the free space in the back row.

'And we'll start.'

Wayne, the senior black belt on the front row, looked round to check the rows were straight and everyone was standing in the right places.

'Class, cheryots! Kyung ye!' he ordered.

Everyone came to attention and bowed.

'Chunbi and relax,' Kai said, smiling again. 'OK, as you all know there was a grading last week and I'm pleased to say that everyone did very well. All those who graded passed and I have your belts and certificates here.'

Relief washed through Gurveer like a warm wave. He had passed. They all had. He suddenly felt about ten feet tall. He was no longer a white belt. Yellow tag sounded so much better.

'In no particular order, Gabriella Fletcher, come forward, please.'

Everyone began to clap as Gabriella ran round to the front of the class.

'Cheryots! Kyung Ye!' Kai ordered, speaking to her alone. 'Well done, Gabriella. You passed with an A star grade. Excellent result – congratulations.'

He removed her white belt and tied a new belt around her waist – still white, but with a yellow stripe that ran along the middle of the full length of the belt. Once he had done this, Kai handed her a certificate and they repeated the formalities of bowing before he called out the next student.

Suddenly it was Gurveer's turn. On hearing his name, he ran out to the front.

'Cheryots! Kyung Ye! Well done, Gurveer. You passed with an A grade. Congratulations.'

An A grade! he thought. *Cool! OK, so Gee got an A star, but an A is still pretty good.*

Two minutes later, his A grade did not feel so good at all. Both Donovan and Abi had also been given A star grades. Of their group of four, he was the only one who had not managed to get the top mark. *Why?* he wondered. It was horrible. For a brief moment he had felt brilliant for having passed with a very good grade, the next he felt like a failure. *What did I do differently from the others? I don't remember making any mistakes.* He replayed the test in his mind, but it didn't help.

It was particularly annoying that Abi had done better than him. When they had started in Kai's class he'd felt that he might finally have found something where he could shine brighter than his little sister. Now that fleeting hope had gone and Abi would get all the glory again. He could already picture his mum and dad making a big deal of that star. They would say nice things to him about his A grade, of course, but once again his little sister's achievement would overshadow his.

Were they really all better than he was? He felt awful.

Chapter 7 – The Stranger

'Are you OK, Gurveer?' Donovan asked, placing an arm across his shoulders. 'Why the glum face? I told you that you'd done well at the grading.'

'I'm sorry,' Gurveer mumbled, looking away. 'I'm just not feeling very well.'

All round the gym their class mates were grabbing their kit and preparing to leave the training hall. Kai was chatting with Marcus and his mum again, handing her information sheets and pointing at particular parts of the paperwork. Trying to avoid meeting the eyes of his friends, Gurveer's gaze drifted up to the windows of the café over the training hall. The man with the dark sunglasses was there. He'd been more subtle this time, sitting tucked in the corner virtually out of sight. Whenever Gurveer looked up he found the man was apparently looking straight at him. Gurveer looked away quickly.

The girls approached.

'Don't all look at once, but have you guys seen the

strange dude up in the café wearing dark glasses?' Abi asked.

Having just looked a moment before, Gurveer was able to keep his focus on Abi. Donovan was not so controlled and to Gurveer's horror, his friend gave a long stare up at the café window before giving a disinterested shrug.

'Can't say I've noticed,' he replied. 'What's the big deal?'

Gurveer's heart started pounding in his chest, the thumping rhythm loud inside his head.

'I noticed him during the training session last week,' she continued. 'I got the feeling he was watching us – not the whole class, just us – but I thought if I said anything you'd think I was crazy.'

'We all think you're crazy anyway,' Gee giggled. 'Why would seeing dark glasses dude make any difference?'

'Thanks, Gee! I love you too,' Abi huffed, pretending to be hurt. 'You know what I mean.'

'Of course I do, babe! Only kidding!'

'Why would he be watching us?' Donovan asked, looking up again. 'He's getting up. It looks like he knows we're on to him. Quick! What should we do? Should we ask him straight?'

'No way!' Gurveer replied quickly. *I'm done for now!* he thought. *He'll make me disappear for sure if he thinks I've pointed him out.* 'Why would you want to talk to him?' he added. 'Just looking at him gives me the creeps.'

'To find out why he's watching us, maybe?' Donovan replied, his voice full of sarcasm.

'Well, I think we should do something,' Abi said. 'Why don't we talk to Kai about him? He'll know what to do.'

'Better do it quickly,' Donovan urged. 'Creepy guy is leaving and Kai is picking up his bags.'

Gurveer held back as the other three ran across the hall to Kai. Would dark glasses guy think he'd blabbed? For a moment he thought he might throw up again.

'Sir! Sir!'

It was too late to stop them now. His fate was sealed.

'Yes, Abi? What is it?'

'Have you noticed the man who's been watching the class from the café this past couple of weeks?'

Kai glanced up at the windows overlooking the training hall.

'No,' he replied. 'What man is that? I don't see anyone.'

'He got up and moved away from the window when he realised we'd spotted him,' Abi said, giving an apologetic shrug.

'What makes you think he's watching you?'

'I don't know,' she admitted. 'It's hard to see

exactly what he's looking at through the dark sunglasses he wears. It's just a feeling. What with those and the long dark coat, he freaks me out.'

'Where is he now?'

'I think he's leaving the building,' Donovan offered. 'He walked off pretty quickly.'

'I want to see this mystery man,' Kai said, striding to the door. 'Come on! We might just catch him. Follow me.'

Gurveer had to run to keep up with Kai and his friends. *I'm toast now for sure,* he thought grimly. *The man will never believe that it wasn't me who told Kai.*

Instinctively completing the ritual courtesy, Kai turned and gave a quick bow to the hall before moving into the reception area. As Gurveer followed, he saw the man leaving through the front doors. He wasn't the only one to spot him.

'There!' Abi called, pointing.

Kai took one look and shouted, 'You! At the door! Stop! I want a word, please.'

The man did not pause. Instead he broke into a run, racing out into the darkness. Kai gave a grunt that could have meant just about anything, but he also started running. He sprinted to the main doors, crashing through them so hard that Gurveer was amazed the glass did not shatter. He watched as Kai paused, momentarily confused as the man had apparently vanished, then a nearby car roared into life and pulled away with tyres squealing in protest.

Kai came back through the entrance doors, his face thoughtful.

'Who was it, sir?' Donovan asked. 'Did you recognise him?'

Kai shook his head.

'I didn't get a good look at him,' he said. 'But I have my suspicions.'

'Should we be worried, sir?' Abi asked, her voice fearful.

'You should be careful,' Kai said slowly. 'I don't think he's about to do anything bad, but let's not take any chances. Come with me. I'm going to drive you home tonight.'

Gurveer's legs felt weak with relief. He felt sure that if he tried to cycle home in the dark, he would be kidnapped and never seen again.

'What about our bikes, sir?' he asked.

'Do you have them chained up outside, Gurveer?'

'Yes, sir.'

'Then leave them there for tonight,' Kai said. 'Come and get them tomorrow after school, preferably before it gets dark.'

'But the man's gone now,' Donovan pointed out. 'I don't see why we can't just ride home together. We should be fine. It's not far and there are four of us, sir.'

Gurveer wanted to scream *'SHUT UP, DONOVAN!'* but his mouth refused to co-operate.

'For my peace of mind, I'd like to take you, Donovan,' Kai explained. 'Once I know you're home safely, I'll do a little investigating and see what I can find out.'

'You said you had suspicions, sir,' Abi prompted. 'Do you know something about him?'

'I *suspect*, but I don't *know*, Abi. And I learned not to jump to conclusions a long time ago,' Kai said firmly. 'There's no need to worry for now. If I'm right, you're not in any immediate danger. Come and put your bags in the car. You can help me carry out the pads as well, if you don't mind.'

Gurveer did as he was told. He desperately wanted to correct his teacher; to tell him that he'd been threatened. That the man was probably going to kidnap him. Again, he found he couldn't speak. He and Donovan each carried a kit bag full of pads out to Kai's Range Rover and placed them in the boot, putting their own bags in alongside. Quick as a flash, Abi hopped into the front seat before any of the others got anywhere close. She turned and gave them a cheeky grin as they climbed into the back.

'You snooze, you lose!' she teased.

Donovan looked a bit irritated, but he climbed into the back without comment. Gurveer didn't care where he sat. He was just relieved that he didn't have to cycle home tonight. Donovan normally assumed leadership of their little group, which Gurveer didn't mind at all, but Abi, despite being a year younger, had always been more of a leader than a follower.

Once they were all in, Kai climbed into the driver's seat and turned his body so he could see all four children.

'Before we go, I have something for you,' he announced.

'For who?' Donovan asked immediately.

'For all of you,' Kai replied. 'Perhaps I should have given you these when you first started training with me, but I wanted to be sure that you were the ones my master spoke about. No harm has been done by delaying.'

Taking his keys from his jacket pocket, Kai leafed through them until he found the one he wanted. He reached across to the passenger glove compartment and unlocked it. All of the children watched as he removed a black box. The box was also locked. Without hesitation Kai singled out a little golden key from his bunch unlike anything they'd ever seen before and inserted it into the lid.

'Here he said,' smiling as he realised all four pairs of eyes were following his every move. 'One for each of you.'

Chapter 8 – The Gift

'Wow!' Gurveer breathed as Kai handed the first of four golden rings to Abi.

'Thank you!' she said, turning the ring this way and that under the dim roof light. It was a delicate band of gold inscribed with strange symbols. 'It's beautiful.'

Kai nodded, handing a similar ring to Gabriella. The rings for the boys were thicker, but similarly covered with unusual markings.

Each in turn gave polite thanks in hushed tones.

'What does the writing say?' Donovan asked.

'I'm not sure,' Kai replied. 'I believe the language is an ancient dialect from a remote region of China. Master Lin told me they will offer you protection. He also said that once accepted, these rings should be worn at all times, though I doubt he was aware of school rules in the UK. You're not supposed to wear jewellery during training either, but I'll make an exception in this case. Wear them as often as you can and keep them close when you can't.'

'Are they like a Celtic knot?' Donovan suggested. 'Mum has several things with Celtic knot designs on that are supposed to ward off sickness and bad luck.'

'Something like that . . .' Kai replied, not meeting his eyes. 'Master Lin was a strange old man. He claimed he could communicate with spirits and powers. I struggled to believe some of the things he told me, but he was a wise man and an amazing martial arts teacher. I learned more from him in the time I was there than I have from anyone in all the years before or since.'

'So did he say anything about what these rings are supposed to protect us from?' Gurveer asked, hoping it would do something to help him keep the man in black away.

'That's a conversation best left for another day,' Kai replied. 'For now, I'd like you all to keep them on day and night. Think of wearing the rings like holding a membership of a special club.'

'Like a secret society,' Gabriella suggested, beaming. 'Cool! It looks a bit big, but. . . whoa!'

'What's the matter, Gee?' Abi asked.

'As I put it on, the ring seemed to shrink to fit my finger,' she said in a dramatic whisper. 'It fits perfectly now.'

'Mine too,' said Donovan, turning his hand and examining the ring closely. 'That's weird!'

'Master Lin was a strange man,' Kai agreed, watching with clear fascination as the children put on the rings.

'They must be magic rings!' Gee announced, her eyes sparkling with excitement.

'Don't get too carried away, Gabriella,' Kai said his face suddenly serious. 'And please don't draw unnecessary attention to them. I don't want you noticed by the wrong people. Although, given that man's reaction when I asked him to stop, I suspect some of those people already know about you.'

The children sat quietly as Kai drove them home in turn. To Gurveer's surprise even Gee, who normally found something to giggle about with Abi, was silent. He and his sister were first to be dropped off.

'Goodnight, sir, and thanks for the lift.'

'My pleasure, Gurveer. Get yourselves inside now. I'll see you all at the next class.'

Donovan and Gee wished them goodnight and waved as the car pulled away. Gurveer lifted a hand in response and then turned towards the door. Kai's car disappeared round the corner and almost immediately a chill ran down Gurveer's spine, causing him to look instinctively up and down the street. He had the distinct feeling someone was watching him, but he could see nothing unusual. Abi opened the front door with her key and stepped inside. Gurveer followed and closed the door quickly behind him.

What a weird evening, he thought.

'Mum! Mum! We passed!' Abi was calling racing ahead into the kitchen.

'That's lovely, darling,' he heard his mother reply. 'Well done. I felt sure you would. Were you given grades, or was it just a pass/fail?'

Gurveer's heart sank. Again, the sensation of failure gripped him. Even though he'd got an 'A' grade, the bitter taste that came with not getting the top 'A*' mark like the others filled his mouth. With all the excitement of the stranger and Kai's gift, he'd temporarily forgotten about his disappointment, but now it was back at full strength.

'Yes. We both did really well. I got an "A*" and Gurveer got an "A".'

There it was. It had been said. He knew the question would come. It was unavoidable. *'Why did you only get an 'A' when your sister scored an 'A*'?'* It was going to be just like school report time. *'You should focus more in class, Gurveer. If you concentrated harder, you could get reports like your sister does, you know?'*

He wanted to slip upstairs to his room without facing his mum, but he didn't get the chance.

'Hello, Gurveer! Well done!' she gushed, pulling him into a hug. 'Abi just told me you did very well. Let's have a look then. Yes. Your new belt looks very fine on you.'

'Thanks, Mum,' he replied, tugging at the ends of the belt to tighten the knot. The material of the belt was very stiff and he'd already had to re-tie it a couple of times as the knot didn't seem to want to stay done up. 'It feels good not to be a total beginner any more. Kai's going to start teaching us lots of new stuff now.'

'Well, be sure to listen well and practise hard and you'll keep doing well,' she said, nodding. 'How did your friends get on?'

'They both passed too,' he said.

'Yes, we all got high grades,' Abi added.

'Excellent! That's a good reflection on your teacher, then. I'm sure he's very proud of you too.'

'Very,' Gurveer agreed.

He glanced across at his sister, who was subconsciously playing with the ring Kai had given her.

'And that's a lovely ring, dear. Where did that come from?'

Gurveer drew a quick breath, convinced that his sister was going to blurt out the whole story, but Abi spoke again before he could say anything.

'Kai gave one to each of his star pupils,' she lied smoothly. 'Look, Gurveer got one as well.'

'How lovely!' his mother replied. 'He's clearly a generous man. Now, children – would you like something to eat? There's some tikka massala in a pot in the oven. The rice will just take a few minutes.'

'That would be great, Mum. I'm starving!'

Mrs Chaudhry laughed. 'I'd be worried if you

weren't, Gurveer. What about you, Abhaya? Will you have some too?'

'Just a little, please, Mum. I never want to eat much after exercising.'

'You eat like a little bird, darling! Very well. Go and get changed, both of you. I don't want you spilling food down your clean white uniforms.'

'Yes, Mum!' they chorused.

'Race you!' Gurveer added, making a break for the stairs.

Abi was after him like a shot. 'You're on,' she replied, and their mother smiled at the thundering sound of feet pounding up the stairs.

'Ah, to be young again,' she sighed and turned back towards the kitchen, shaking her head and smiling.

Chapter 9 – Grumpy-chops

'Oh for goodness' sake, Gurveer!' Donovan sighed the following Tuesday, punching him lightly on the arm as they walked out of the school gates and set off for home. 'Cheer up, it's nearly Christmas! What's got into you this week? You've had a face as long as Eeyore for most of it. Anyone would think the world was about to end!'

'I'm sorry,' he replied, unable to look his friend in the eye. 'Christmas doesn't really hold the same excitement for us. We don't make a big deal of it in our house. Divali on the other hand . . .'

Looking along the street Gurveer felt like the Grinch for even suggesting he wasn't looking forward to Christmas. Everywhere he looked there were twinkling lights. The whole neighbourhood seemed to have draped lights across the outsides of their houses and the street was ablaze with a mass of blinking, twinkling, sparkling colour, even though it was not yet fully dark.

'Well we're barely doing any work in school and we

haven't had homework for ages,' Donovan pointed out, changing tack. Given how good a friend Gurveer was, he felt embarrassed about how little he knew of his friend's religion and traditions and made a silent decision to start finding out. 'It's tae kwon-do tonight. Aren't you looking forwards to our first proper lesson as yellow tags?'

'He's still being a grumpy-chops because he didn't get an 'A*' at the grading last week,' Abi called from behind them.

'Seriously?' Donovan asked, his voice rising with surprise. He looked across at his friend. 'You've got to be kidding! That's the most ridiculous thing I've ever heard! You did really well.'

'He's been sore about it ever since we got our grades,' Abi explained. 'Probably because I always beat him at everything.'

'But it could so easily have been the other way round, Gurveer,' Donovan said, ignoring the second part of Abi's explanation. 'Chatting to some of the other students, they say the margin between an A and an A* is really small. It could easily be you getting the A* next time and the rest of us getting jealous.'

'Huh! Fat chance!' Gurveer huffed. It was true that his result bugged him, but that wasn't the whole story. In truth he was scared, but despite them all being aware of the watcher in black, he still couldn't bring himself to tell them about his encounter in the alleyway and keeping the secret was eating him up inside.

Gabriella giggled, drawing a stern look from Donovan. 'He really is a grumpy-chops, isn't he?' she said, her eyes glittering with amusement.

'You're not helping, Gee!' Donovan called over his shoulder, turning to frown at her. He turned back to his friend. 'Come on, Gurveer! You're easily as good as the rest of us. In fact I'd love to be able to punch as hard as you do.'

'You're just saying that to make me feel good,' Gurveer replied. He looked at Donovan with narrowed eyes. 'Don't bother. It doesn't matter.'

'Of course it matters!' Donovan insisted. 'I'm serious. I have no idea why the three of us got A*s and you didn't, Gurveer, but it's not down to your ability, I promise you. Sure, Gee can kick higher than any of us, but aside from the leg raises there were no kicks in the exam, so she didn't have a chance to show off her flexibility. But you have the hardest punches. Are you sure you were punching at full power during the test?'

'Yes . . . well, no . . .' Gurveer admitted, thinking back again to the exam and trying to remember. 'I was concentrating more on doing everything correctly.'

'There it is, then!' Donovan explained. 'Don't you remember what Kai said? You've got to give each move one hundred per cent. I put everything I had behind every punch and block. If you had something in reserve, the examiner must have picked up on that. It doesn't mean you're not as good as we are. You passed, just like we did. The grade you got isn't printed on your belt, so nobody looking at us in class will ever know.'

'Yes, but I know,' he replied stubbornly.

An awkward silence fell between them and Gurveer thought about what Donovan had said for a moment. Could he be right? Could the difference between their marks have been something so simple? It was true – he had been a grump over the results, but he didn't feel he could tell them that his mood was more to do with his fear of the stranger. His eyebrows drew together in a fierce frown as he tried to remember the test more clearly. It had all happened so fast.

I don't want to drive Donovan away. I should apologise. I should tell him the truth.

Gurveer turned to Donovan with the intention of putting his fear aside and explaining, but as he did so something caught his eye that made his breath freeze in his throat.

'Don't look now, but we're being followed again,' he muttered.

'Zach?' Donovan asked, resisting the urge to look over his shoulder.

'No,' Gurveer said, his gut churning. 'Dark glasses guy. Other side of the street about a hundred metres back.'

Donovan's brows drew into a frown. 'I'm amazed he can see where he's going wearing those glasses. What do you think? Should we make a run for it?'

'I don't know. It would be a bit obvious. What do you think, girls?' he asked, glancing over his shoulder at his sister. He slowed his pace a little to allow the girls to close the gap between them. As they caught up, Gabriella flashed a frightened glance over her shoulder.

'He's strange!' she muttered. 'What do you think he wants?'

'No idea,' Gurveer breathed. 'It's daylight. There're four of us. Surely we're safe so long as we stick together.'

'I get the feeling Kai knows him. If he's as good at martial arts as Kai, he could easily hurt us all,' Abi pointed out. 'But why would he want to? We haven't done anything to him.'

It was a good question. Gurveer fingered his ring as he considered it.

'I want to run,' Gabriella said, clearly scared. 'I definitely don't want him getting any closer. Even knowing he's back there freaks me out. Maybe we should ring someone – the police? I've got my mobile.'

'And tell them what, Gee?' Donovan asked. 'Hello Mr. Policeman. Can you come and arrest a man wearing dark glasses because he looks creepy and we think he's following us. Our parents might get into trouble for us wasting police time.'

Gurveer had a better idea.

'To be honest, Donovan, I'd rather be in trouble with the police for making a mistake than face that guy,' he said. 'Remember what we were taught about "stranger danger" in school? But rather than risk getting into trouble, why don't we ring Kai? I've got his mobile number in my phone.'

'Brilliant!' Donovan said enthusiastically. 'Do it. He'll know what to do. Let's just keep walking for now.

Gurveer pulled his phone out of his pocket and slid the cover clear to reveal the screen. A few seconds later he'd found the number he wanted, selected it, and put the phone to his ear.

'It's ringing,' he told them.

They all waited, huddling close in the hope that they might hear what Kai said. Gurveer held the phone slightly away from his ear so they could all hear the faint *burrp burrp . . . burrp burrp* sound of the ringing tone. He wasn't answering. Suddenly it connected.

'Kai?' Gurveer said, pulling the phone closer to his ear as his chest tightened with excitement. 'Hello, Kai . . .'

Suddenly Kai's voice cut in on the other end of the line. *'You're through to Kai Green's phone. I'm sorry, but I can't answer right now. Leave a message after the tone and I'll get back to you as soon as I can.'*

Gurveer lowered the phone from his ear and pressed the disconnect button.

'Answer-phone,' he muttered.

'Great!' Abi exclaimed. 'Now what do we do?'

Chapter 10 – The Fight

'He's not doing us any harm at the moment,' Abi said. 'Let's not panic. We'll take it in turns to keep an eye on him and just keep walking.'

Gurveer looked at his little sister with a mixture of surprise and respect. She sounded so calm and grown up.

Donovan nodded. 'Yes. Try to act as if we haven't seen him,' he added in a low voice. 'We don't want to spook him into action.'

'What if he's not alone?' Gabriella asked.

'I was hoping you wouldn't think of that,' Abi replied. 'Just keep your eyes peeled for anything unusual and keep walking. We shouldn't take the alleyway tonight. Let's stick to the roads.'

'Sounds like a plan,' Donovan said. He tried to look casual. 'So have any of you looked ahead at what we'll be learning in class tonight?' he asked.

'The first proper pattern, I imagine,' Gabriella replied. 'I had a quick look on YouTube a couple of days ago. It's called Chon Ji and there are nineteen moves.'

'I did the same,' Donovan admitted. 'I didn't think it looked much more difficult than the exercise we did for our first belt.'

How can they talk about tae kwon-do lessons at a time like this? Gurveer wondered. *But that was so like Donovan – single-minded and always several steps ahead. It felt wrong, but he decided he had better join in.*

'I'm just going to wait and let Kai teach me,' he mumbled. 'I don't want to get any wrong ideas in my head from watching people online. There're loads of different styles of tae kwon-do out there. I'm not going to start self-teaching stuff, because I bet that if I did, I'd learn something that was out of date, or a different style.'

'Pick up the pace, boys,' Abi warned in a low voice. 'Our tail is catching up.'

'Race you to the door!' Gabriella shouted suddenly, barging past the boys and sprinting off down the road. 'You boys are so slow you couldn't catch a cold!' she added in a jeering voice.

Nice touch! Gurveer thought, unable to keep the corners of his mouth from twitching up in the hint of a smile.

Abi was quickest to follow. The two boys glanced at each other for a split second before racing after the two girls.

'You're on!' Donovan shouted after them.

Gurveer didn't add anything. He concentrated on running. His running had been improving since he started the tae kwon-do training three months earlier. He looked back. The shadowy figure on the other side of the road was also now running silently along the pavement.

'Donovan!'

'I see him,' he replied. 'Keep running. Don't cross.'

'But he'll cut us off,' Gurveer panted. 'He's faster.'

'Then we'll turn down the next alley.'

'Whatever you say.'

They were approaching the end of the street when the man in the dark glasses angled across the road, accelerating to intercept them. Suddenly there was a screech of tyres and Kai's Range Rover appeared from behind them and pulled to a noisy stop on the other side of the street. Kai leapt out.

'Kai!' Gurveer exclaimed.

'Keep running,' he ordered.

The man in the dark glasses slowed; his running pace stuttering. His hesitation was enough for Kai to get in front of him. The man slowed further until he came to a stop just a few paces from the martial arts instructor.

'Move out of my way, Kai,' he warned.

'So you know who I am,' Kai acknowledged.

Gurveer's curiosity got the better of him. The girls were racing away and Donovan was following, but

79

Gurveer slowed to a stop, pretending to be out of breath. He turned to see what was happening.

'Gurveer!' Donovan called over his shoulder. 'Kai told us to keep going.'

But when he saw the two men facing one another, he also slowed to a stop. The girls kept running.

'I know who you work for,' Kai said, his voice calm. 'Tell your master the children are protected. There's nothing for you here.'

'I mean no harm to the children,' the man said. 'I wanted to ask them a few questions, that's all.'

'Don't listen to him, Kai,' Gurveer shouted in his mind. *'He's lying!'*

'Really?' Kai replied, his voice thick with sarcasm. 'You have a strange way of approaching children. Don't you know they're taught not to speak with strangers? The dark coat and glasses alone would set off alarm bells with even the most backward of youngsters and there's nothing backward about these four.'

'You're so distrustful, Kai!' the man said. He opened his mouth as if he was going to continue speaking, but instead he launched a vicious kick at Kai's groin.

Gurveer felt a sudden pulse of heat in his right hand.

'Whoa!' he exclaimed.

'Ow!' Donovan muttered at precisely the same moment.

The boys looked at one another – scared. Together they raised their right hands to look at their rings. Both were giving off a faint glowing light.

'What's happening?' Gurveer gasped.

'I've no idea,' Donovan replied, walking back towards him. 'Did your ring just get hot?'

'Yeah.'

The man's attack on Kai was sudden and so quick that Gurveer, momentarily distracted by his ring barely saw him move. To his amazement, he realised Kai had blocked the kick and struck back so fast the man had not seen the blow coming.

Replaying the scene in his mind, he realised that as the man's foot had swung up, Kai's fists had instinctively thrust down, crossing in front of his body to form an X shape with his lower arms. All the force of the rising foot had been absorbed by Kai's wrists as it struck the centre of the X. Quick as a flash, Kai had pulled back his fists into a guard and lashed out with his right hand, connecting the man's face hard with a back-fist strike that sent his dark glasses flying off into the road.

There was no more chat. Kai was in a fighting stance, moving on the balls of his feet, his fists up in a guard and his body turned side on to his opponent.

The man in the dark coat attacked again, flashing up a side kick. Kai brushed it aside and spun inside the man's guard to hammer a reverse side kick of his own up into the man's ribs before dancing away out of reach again. The man grunted at the impact his face twisting with pain and anger.

He came forward again and there was another rapid exchange. From what Gurveer could see the man was quick, but his movements were being hampered by the length of his dark coat. Kai, however, was dressed in a track suit with an open fleece over the top and his movements were fluid and unrestricted. Again Kai landed a telling blow, this time with a turning kick to the stomach. The thudding sound of the impact made Gurveer wince.

'That had to hurt,' he muttered.

'Too right!' Donovan replied. 'I wouldn't want to be on the end of one of Kai's kicks.'

The man in the dark coat backed away warily. He was giving up. Gurveer could see it in his expression. He'd lost confidence. Kai was too fast for him.

'Another time, Kai,' he growled at the martial arts instructor.

'Stay away from the children,' Kai responded calmly, maintaining his fighting stance and ignoring the man's threatening tone. 'Give your master the same message. My students are protected. If you try anything foolish again, I'll find him and take it up with him personally.'

'My master doesn't take kindly to threats, Kai. You should know that,' the man said, still retreating.

'It wasn't a threat. It was a promise.'

The man turned and ran into the dusky half-light, angling across the road and quickly becoming little more than a fleeing shadow.

Gurveer could feel his ring cooling the further away the man went.

Kai turned to face them, his expression angry.

'Why are you still here? Next time I tell you to do something, you do it – straight away! No questions, no hesitation,' he snapped. 'Do you understand?'

Gurveer nodded and mumbled an apology, but to Gurveer's surprise Donovan held his ground, his dark eyes narrowing as he met Kai's angry gaze with a hard stare of his own.

'Yes, sir, I understand, but what's with these rings?' Donovan asked boldly, holding up his ring finger towards Kai. 'Look! They're still glowing and they got really hot just now. It was freaky!'

'I told you before, Donovan – I don't know anything about the rings. If they have some strange power, it is beyond my understanding. Master Lin did not choose to share their secret with me.'

'So . . .'

'Tonight! After class,' Kai said firmly. 'I'll see you and the girls then, and we'll talk it through.'

'Yes, sir.'

Chapter 11 – 'You're not ready'

The lesson was nearly finished. Gurveer was so curious to find out what Kai was going to tell them afterwards that he was having difficulty concentrating. All round the sports hall students were in small groups, each being led by a black belt. Gurveer, Donovan, Gabriella and Abi were being taught by Kai.

'Check your stances!' Kai ordered, snapping him back to the present. 'Gurveer, that's not 'L' stance. You, too, Abi. Both of you move more weight on to your back foot – that's it. Lower, Donovan – bend those legs. Now lengthen the stance a little – good.'

Gurveer did his best to do what Kai was telling him, but his mind was still caught up with the strange events of the afternoon.

'That's better, Gurveer. Good, Donovan. Excellent, Abi!' Kai approved. 'It takes a bit of getting used to, but this is much closer to a fighting stance than anything you've learned so far. Your body is sideways on to your opponent, giving him less target area to aim at, and you're better balanced for both attack and defence. OK . . . EVERYONE – BARROL!'

All of the students in the sports hall stopped what they were doing and returned to ready stance, waiting for the next order.

'We're out of time, people. Make the rows up. Quick as you can! Five . . . four . . .'

Everyone scrambled for position, but by the time Kai's countdown reached one everyone was standing in lines, ready and waiting. Gurveer could feel where his thighs and shoulders would ache in the morning. The class had been difficult, with several new techniques to remember, but to his intense relief there had been no sign of the stranger up in the cafe.

'And we'll finish.'

The senior black belt looked round to make sure everyone was in position before calling out 'Class, cheryots! Kyung Ye!'

Everyone made attention stance, bowed and scattered, all clapping and calling out 'Thank you, sir!' Kai gave Donovan, Gurveer and the girls a meaningful look. Gurveer's chest tightened, making it suddenly hard to breathe.

'Come on,' he muttered to Donovan. 'Maybe now we'll get some answers.'

They said goodbye to Marcus, who was looking exhausted, but proud to be wearing a white belt over his T-shirt. Then they helped Kai gather the focus pads into the bags and carried them out to his car. Once all the equipment was stacked in the boot, the instructor indicated for them to climb into the car. Donovan took the front passenger seat this time, while Gurveer and the girls climbed into the back. Kai jumped into the driver's seat and closed the door. For a moment he didn't say anything. He just looked at them, his eyes switching from face to face and pausing. His look was intense, as if he was searching for something.

'OK, kids,' Kai began. 'I've had a bit of time to think about what happened this afternoon. I'll be honest: events are moving much faster than I expected.'

'Who is that man, Kai?' Gabriella asked, her voice frightened. 'The boys said you knew him.'

'I don't know him personally,' Kai corrected, shaking his head. 'But I don't need to. I know who he's working for, which is more important. We'll need to be careful. You're not ready to tangle with him and you won't be ready for a long time yet. You've barely begun your training. He knows this, but he's also not sure yet if you're the four my master saw in his vision. I don't think he'll make any real moves until he's certain, but he's not the most predictable person I've met.'

'I . . . I'm not so sure,' Gurveer stammered.

'What do you mean, Gurveer?'

'That man grabbed me from behind when I was on

my way home from the Leisure Centre after the Tuesday lesson last week. He warned me that if I told you about him, he would make me disappear. I know it was Abi who told you, but I think he was after me today.'

Kai and the others all looked at him with shocked expressions.

'You've kept this to yourself all week?' Donovan said, his voice full of amazement. 'I knew there was something wrong, but I thought it was just the grading.'

'He will not take you, Gurveer,' Kai assured him. 'My friends and I will be protecting you at all times from now on. You should stay alert, but don't worry. I'm not going to let anything happen to you.'

For Gurveer it was as if a weight had been lifted from his heart. He felt dizzy with relief. He had finally managed to tell someone and it felt good to get his fear out in the open.

'I'm also going to teach all of you some techniques to get free from someone who grabs you from behind,' he added. 'But I don't want to do that in class. It would be too obvious. We had better meet somewhere else for that lesson.'

'Who do you think he's working for, Kai?' Donovan asked. 'And why did our rings get hot and glow when you got in that fight earlier? The girls say they didn't notice anything strange, but both Gurveer and me felt and saw our rings react when that man attacked you.'

'He works for a man called Chen Gwang Hai. He was one of the other students in the monastery where I trained in the Far East. To begin with we were friends, but then I discovered he had a dark secret. When I revealed this secret to my master, Chen fled. How he had hidden his true nature from my Master for so long, I don't know. Master Lin seemed to have a sixth sense when it came to judging character, but his instinct failed him with Chen. The man is a snake worshipper and worse.'

'Snakes?' Gurveer said, giving a shudder. 'Eurgh!'

'The snakes are not what you need to worry about,' Kai warned. 'These people are part of a dark cult whose followers have some very strange beliefs. But don't be afraid. I've arranged a team to protect you. We will see to it that Chen and his people will not harm you.'

'And the rings?' Donovan persisted. 'What about the rings?'

'Now that *is* a mystery,' Kai admitted. 'Master Lin told me they would offer you protection, but he didn't explain how, or what form that protection would take. To be honest I thought they were simply a sort of lucky charm, but my old Master was a strange man with some very unusual abilities. Did it hurt when they got hot?'

Gurveer thought for a moment.

'No, he replied. 'I think I cried out more with surprise than anything else.'

Donovan nodded.

'Same,' he said.

'I suppose it shouldn't surprise me that there's more to the rings than meets the eye. More than ever now, I encourage you to wear them at all times. But I'll say it again – even if the rings offer some sort of protection that I don't understand, don't try anything stupid. If someone threatens you – just run! Do you understand?'

'Yes, Kai,' they chorused.

'Are you sure?' he asked.

'Yes, sir.'

'Then why didn't you run when I told you to this afternoon, boys?'

'It won't happen again, Kai,' Gurveer promised. 'Sorry. I know I'm not as good as the others at tae kwon-do, but I promise I'll listen from now on.'

Kai stared at Gurveer for a moment.

'What gave you the idea that you're not as good as the others?' he asked.

'He's sore because we all got A*s and he didn't' Abi explained. 'He's been sulking ever since we got the grading results.'

'Abi! I have not!' Gurveer protested.

'Yes you have!'

'Woah! Both of you,' Kai ordered. 'First – you four need to think like a team. You were each named after a warrior. Support one another and you'll *all* be stronger for it. Gurveer, you **are** just as good as the rest of these guys. You each have different strengths and weaknesses, but I wouldn't hold any of you above the others in ability – at least not at the moment.'

'But if that's the case, sir, why. . .'

'I watched the grading alongside the examiner,' Kai interrupted, holding up his hand to stop Gurveer from finishing his question. 'The only difference I could see between you and the others was the tightness in your shoulders, which I put down to a bit of nerves. Your techniques are strong, Gurveer. Don't doubt yourself. In class you do just as well as the others. . . when you're not daydreaming and off in your own little world that is! Relax. Listen. Learn. Do this and you'll perform every bit as well as they do at the next grading.'

'See! I told you . . .' Donovan began.

Again Kai held up his hand for silence.

'You're *all* doing well, but you're still beginners and you're young,' he said, his voice serious. 'Work hard and you'll become talented martial artists. However, you're not ready to fight any battles yet. You must stay alert, and I will too. Chen and his people are aware of you, but they're not sure what to make of you yet. The longer we can keep them in the dark about your progress, the better.'

Kai's words of warning were serious, but Gurveer barely heard them. Despite the instructor's warning about day-dreaming his mind had wandered and a fierce heat surged through his body. There had been no falseness in his instructor's voice. Kai meant it. He was as good as the others. He felt silly for having got so grumpy about the grades. Kai believed in him. Donovan and the girls respected him as their equal. Suddenly he felt strong. Perhaps he should feel scared of this man, Chen, but his fear had dissolved with Kai's words. It was as if something inside him had clicked into place.

It's all too easy to shrink with disappointment, he realised. I should have used my feelings to fuel my motivation and try even harder. I allowed my fear to cripple me. Kai is right. None of us are warriors yet, but if we work hard then one day we could be: I could be. And I'm going to practise night and day until I am . . .

* * * * *

'Yes, Driss. What is it?'

'Kai knows, Master,' he replied, so nervous that his tongue felt too big for his mouth.

'Knows what?'

'That I've been watching the kids,' Driss admitted, his body tense and his ribs aching from where he had been kicked. 'He . . . spoke to me today. He knows about you and asked me to warn you to stay away from them.'

Driss expected an explosion of anger. It didn't come. To his surprise, Master Chen's face showed no emotion as he considered this news.

'It was to be expected, I suppose,' he said. 'Kai is no fool. If he believes these children are the four he's been expecting, he will be monitoring them closely. Let him. There is no rush. The serum is still not ready

– there have been . . . complications. Let Kai stew for a while. Continue to watch the children from a distance, but don't make any moves yet.'

'Yes, Master,' Driss replied, unable to completely hide his relief.

'We will let Kai tire of watching them and then strike when he least expects it.'

Look out for *Warrior Kids 3 – Kicking up a Storm*

www.markrobsonauthor.com